Grandma's Garden

Elaine Moore

Grandma's Garden

pictures by Dan Andreasen

Lothrop, Lee & Shepard Books   New York

First Edition   1   2   3   4   5   6   7   8   9   10

Library of Congress Cataloging in Publication Data
Moore, Elaine.   Grandma's garden / by Elaine Moore ; illustrations by Dan Andreasen
p.   cm.   Summary: Kim visits Grandma in the spring to help her plant her garden.
ISBN 0-688-08693-4—ISBN 0-688-08694-2 (lib. bdg.).   [1. Gardening—Fiction.
2. Grandmothers—Fiction.]   I. Andreasen, D., ill.   II. Title.   PZ7.M7832Gp   1990
[E]—dc20   90-6052   CIP   AC

For Devon
and for Pop-Pop,
who saved the plums for Devon
E.M.

For Ann and Emily
D.A.

Kim

WHEN I FIRST WAKE UP, I think I'm in my bed at home. Then I hear squirrels chattering outside the window. I smell bacon sizzling, and I remember I'm at Grandma's. It is spring, and I have come to help Grandma wake her garden.

I can't wait to see the garden. I eat breakfast quickly and help Grandma clean up. Then I grab her hand and pull her outside.

When I see the plum trees we planted last summer, I am disappointed. "Oh, Grandma," I say. "They didn't grow much at all."

"Don't worry," Grandma tells me. "Last month these trees were loaded with blossoms. Now look. See all these teeny tiny plums? This summer we'll have too many plums to count."

I hardly recognize Grandma's garden. In summer it has
rows of green leaves and vines. In winter it disappears under
the snow. Now it's just a big bare patch of brown dirt.

Grandma breaks the hard clumps with her hoe. I help
her rake the dirt smooth and even. When Grandma ties
twine to a stick at the garden's edge, it is my job to walk
lightly across to the other side. I loop the twine around
another stick. Now we'll be able to plant our seeds in
straight rows.

Grandma gives me a catalogue to look at while she fixes lunch. I see a giant pumpkin and a sunflower as tall as a barn.

"Look, Grandma!" I say. "Let's plant these!"

"It's too early for pumpkins and sunflowers," says Grandma. "Here's what we're going to plant today."

She gives me a handful of little envelopes. One has a picture of something I don't like, peas. Three have pictures of leafy green lettuce, and another a picture of a carrot. The last has bright red radishes.

I carefully tear a corner off the radish envelope and pour some tiny black dots into my hand. "Are these little things radish seeds?" I ask.

"Yes," says Grandma. "And carrots are bigger than radishes, but their seeds are even smaller."

After lunch we go out to plant the seeds. "Radishes and carrots make good partners in a garden," Grandma says. "The fast-growing radishes will help loosen the soil for the slower-growing carrots."

Following the string, Grandma sprinkles carrot seeds. I follow her along the rows, planting radishes. I pat the soil lightly with my hand. Then, while Grandma rolls up the string, I mark the rows with the empty seed packets.

"We make good partners too, Grandma," I say.

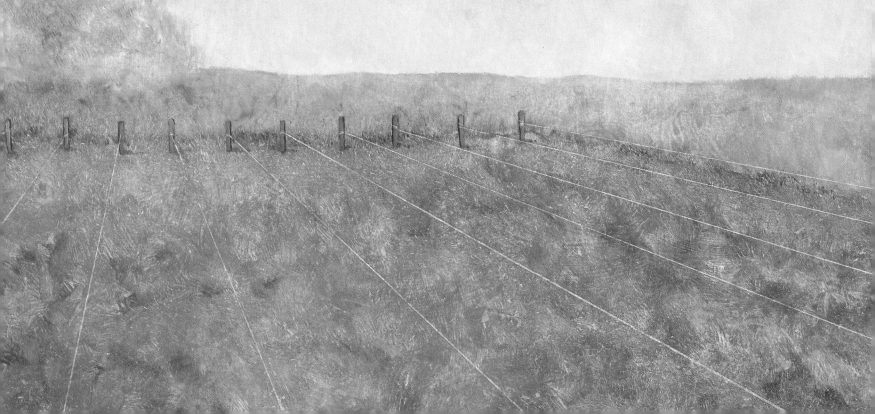

Next, Grandma and I make a scarecrow. We take old clothes out of the attic and stuff them with straw. Then we top him with a floppy hat. We hope he will frighten away the birds who want to eat our seeds.

After supper, Grandma and I are tired. I barely finish my ice cream before I tumble into bed.

Later, I am suddenly awake. I know it is only thunder, but I am frightened. I call Grandma.

"Don't worry, Kim," she says. "The thunder and lightning are far away, and now the rain's starting—hear it? Rain will help our garden. It will give the vegetables a good start."

We listen to the rain on the roof. Grandma stays with me till I fall asleep.

When I get up the next morning, the rain has stopped, but I can't see the garden. All I can see is a big brown lake.

"You were wrong, Grandma!" I say. "The rain ruined our garden. Look, our markers are gone."

"Yes, and the seeds have been washed away, too," Grandma tells me. "But you'll see, the sun will come out and the ground will dry. We'll plant more seeds and make new markers."

I am still sad, but then Grandma says, "Feel that wind! I was hoping for a day like this. There's something special we can do on a windy day."

"I know!" I shout. "A kite!"

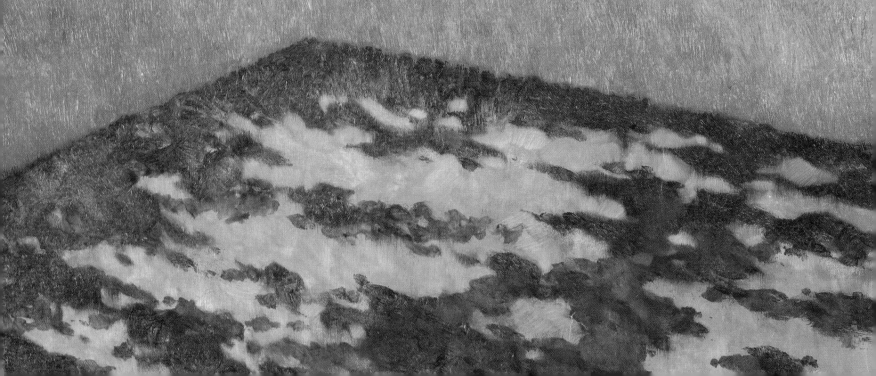

Grandma and I climb the hill together. The paper
kite makes a loud crackling noise and rears back from
Grandma's hand. "Hold tight to the string," Grandma
calls. "Now give it a little jerk."

"Let go, Grandma!" I shout, and the kite whips free in
the wind.

We take turns holding the string and guiding the kite.
I make it fly high over Grandma's house.

After dinner I color and paste while Grandma listens to
the radio. All at once Grandma stands up. "Did you hear
that?" she says. "There's a frost warning on for tonight.
Frost could hurt our plums."

"Oh, no," I groan. Grandma is putting on her coat.
"Grandma, what are we going to do?"

"We're going to fool Jack Frost," she says. "Come on."

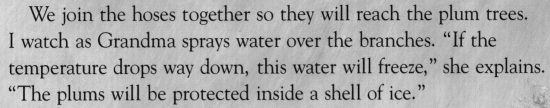

We join the hoses together so they will reach the plum trees. I watch as Grandma sprays water over the branches. "If the temperature drops way down, this water will freeze," she explains. "The plums will be protected inside a shell of ice."

I'm still afraid the frost will get our plums. "How do you know that will work?" I ask.

"I don't," Grandma answers. "But I can make a pretty good guess, and we can hope."

Before I go to bed, I look out at the plum trees. Covered with ice, they sparkle like fiery stars. Grandma was wrong about the rain. I hope she is right about the plums.

In the morning the sun shines on the dripping plum trees. Where the ice has melted, I see teeny tiny plums.

"Hurray!" I shout. "Too many plums to count!"

Grandma laughs. "Now, if we want those vegetables, we'd better plant some more seeds," she says.

Grandma and I mark new rows. We are nearly finished planting new seeds when I tell Grandma, "I wish I could be here to help pick the radishes."

"So do I, Kim," says Grandma. "But the carrots will be ready when you're back in July."

I stare at the bare ground. "Grandma, that's too long."

Grandma puts her arms around me. "It does seem long, but it'll be summer before you know it. Besides, I know a way to make the time pass even quicker."

I watch as Grandma puts some soil in a jar
for me to take home.

"You can plant radishes and carrots in a
flowerpot on your windowsill," Grandma says.
"When you pick your radishes, you can think of
me picking mine. And when the carrot greens
stand as tall as your finger, it will be summer."

Summer, I think. That's when I come back
to Grandma's.

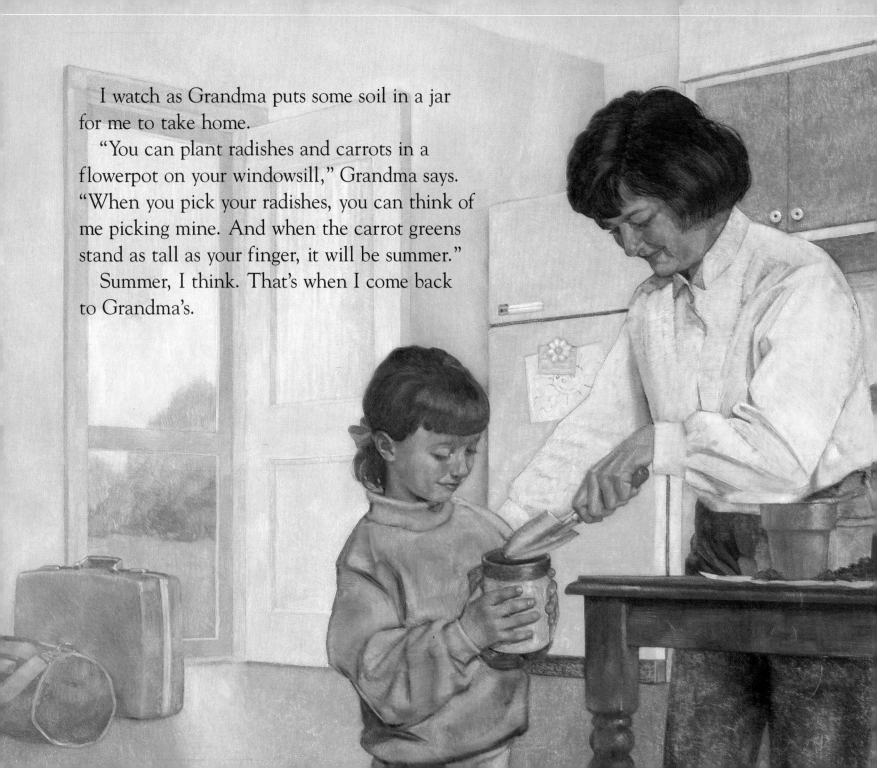